STAR BABY

by Margaret O'Hair

Clarion Books
New York

Illustrated by
Erin Eitter Kono

Clarion Books
a Houghton Mifflin Company imprint
215 Park Avenue South, New York, NY 10003
Text copyright © 2005 by Margaret O'Hair
Illustrations copyright © 2005 by Erin Eitter Kono

The illustrations were executed in acrylic on watercolor paper.
The text was set in 37-point Stellar.

www.houghtonmifflinbooks.com

Printed in Singapore

Library of Congress Cataloging-in-Publication Data

O'Hair, Margaret.
Star baby / by Margaret O'Hair ; illustrated by Erin Eitter Kono.
p. cm.
Summary: Easy-to-read, rhyming text explores the world of babies, as they do such things as
point, scoot, rock, and hug.
ISBN 0-618-30668-4
[1. Babies—Fiction. 2. Stories in rhyme.] I. Kono, Erin Eitter, ill. II. Title.
PZ8.3.O353St 2005
[E]—dc22
                            2004016187

ISBN-13: 978-0-618-30668-8
ISBN-10: 0-618-30668-4

TWP 10 9 8 7 6 5 4 3 2 1

For my stars,
Sam and Stephanie
—M.O.

For my sister Nina
—E.E.K.

Hi, baby
Up, baby
Sun, baby
Shine

5

Smile, baby
Laugh, baby
Hug, baby
Mine

6

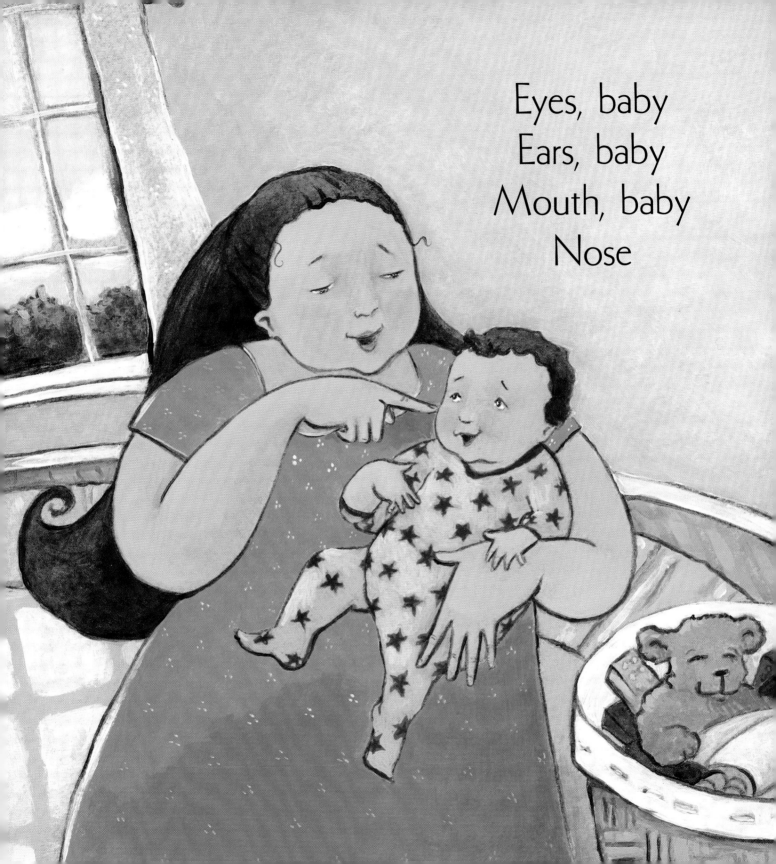

Eyes, baby
Ears, baby
Mouth, baby
Nose

Point, baby
Touch, baby
Count, baby
Toes

8

Hide, baby
Seek, baby
Peek, baby
Boo

10

Where, baby?
What, baby?
Who, baby?
You!

11

Scoot, baby
Crawl, baby
Go, baby
Go!

Wait, baby
Wait, baby
Wait, baby
No!

13

Lunch, baby
Crunch, baby
Eat, baby
Burp

Sip, baby
Slop, baby
Drink, baby
Slurp

15

Sweet, baby
Yawn, baby
Here, baby
Bear

16

Rock, baby
Rest, baby
Nap, baby
There

17

Reach, baby
Pull, baby
Yes, baby
Stand

18

Walk, baby
Oops! baby
Here, baby
Hand

19

Spoon, baby
Pot, baby
Bang, baby
Boom

20

Car, baby
Boat, baby
Truck, baby
Zoom

21

Swing, baby
Swoosh, baby
Soar, baby
High

Bath, baby
Splash, baby
Rub, baby
Dry

25

Phone, baby
Talk, baby
Laugh, baby
Look

27

Read, baby
Clap, baby
More, baby
Book

29

Hug, baby
Love, baby
Wish, baby
Kiss

31

Night, baby
Moon, baby
Star, baby
Bliss